FIG STREET KIDS

1

SERIES

Tommy's Clubhouse

7

Books by Sharon Hambrick

The Arby Jenkins Series
    Arby Jenkins
    Arby Jenkins, Mighty Mustangs
    Arby Jenkins, Ready to Roll
    Stuart's Run to Faith
    Arby Jenkins Meets His Match
The Year of Abi Crim
Adoniram Judson: God's Man in Burma
The Fig Street Kids Series
    Tommy's Clubhouse

FIG STREET KIDS SERIES 1

Tommy's Clubhouse

BOYS ARE GREAT, AND GIRLS ARE NOT

By Sharon Hambrick

JOURNEY FORTH™

Greenville, South Carolina

Library of Congress Cataloging-in-Publication Data

Hambrick, Sharon, 1961-
  Tommy's clubhouse / by Sharon Hambrick ; illustrated by
Maurie J. Manning
      p. cm.—(The Fig Street kids ; bk. 1)
Summary: Tommy and his friends start a club that
eventually does good deeds in his neighborhood.
  ISBN 1-57924-993-0 (pbk. : alk. paper)
  [1. Clubs—Fiction. 2. Neighborhood—Fiction.] I.
Manning, Maurie, ill. II. Title.
  PZ7.H1755To 2003
  [Fic]—dc21

                                        2003009989

Designed by Jon Kopp
Illustrations by Maurie J. Manning
Composition by Melissa Matos

© 2003 BJU Press
Greenville, SC 29614

ISBN 1-57924-993-0

15 14 13 12 11 10 9 8 7 6 5 4 3 2 1

To Karen Yamaki
with admiration

Contents

1
Boys Are Great

My name is Thomas Arthur Jackson, but my friends call me Tommy. I'm seven years old, and I'm the president of the Boys Are Great Club.

Our club doesn't allow any girls to be members unless they are willing to say the motto, which is this: "Boys are great, and girls are not great." So far no girls are coming to join.

My big sister's name is Penny. She tried to start a Girls Are Great Club, but when she made up her flyers, she noticed the initials were GAG, so she threw them all away. Mom said that was a waste of color ink and printer paper.

I told Penny at dinner time that the GAG thing proves what I've been saying all along about girls. They can't even get their initials straight. Mom said I should speak nicely to my sister and also I should eat my peas.

I said I don't like peas, but Mom said I should do what I'm told or I'll end up like her brother, Uncle Mick.

I asked what would be wrong with that.

"He's loud and lazy," Mom said.

"Do you love him?" Penny said.

"Of course I love him, but he's loud and lazy."

I said, "How loud? How lazy? Does he sleep all day? Does he shout?"

Mom said to eat my peas, and she didn't want to have to tell me again!

I started mashing the peas into a green blob on my plate, and then I poked holes in my smooshy pea-pile with my fork. Then, after a minute I thought of something supersmart. I said if he sleeps all day, maybe he has sleeping sickness.

"Hey, I'm getting that sickness too!" I said. "I'm so sleepy, I'm going to fall out of my chair. I'm so sleepy, I can't eat my peas!"

Mom turned around and walked over to me. Very quietly she said, "Son, you will now eat your peas while I watch you."

After I finished my peas, I said, "How loud is Uncle Mick? Does he always shout? Even on the telephone? Did he make someone go deaf? Does he yell like this?" Right there I started to yell really loud like this: "ya-ya-ya-ya-ya!!!" as loud as I could.

I ran around yelling for a minute, and then I sat back down and said, "Now I know why Uncle Mick is so sleepy. It's hard to run and yell for a long time."

Dad said, "Hmmm," and looked at me funny. Mom came over and ruffled up my hair, so I knew it was sticking straight up. She kissed me and said, "Your turn to wash. Penny dries."

Me and Penny did the dishes, and I only yelled a few times just to see how it feels to be like Uncle Mick. I couldn't do the lazy part though, because

Mom said I should do my homework instead of having sleeping sickness.

I yelled a few times while I wrote some plusses. One plus one and one plus two all the way up to one plus nine.

2
Howie and Zack

My best friends are Howie Miller and Zack Oliver. Every day they come to my backyard clubhouse after school. Our clubhouse is the greatest clubhouse I've ever seen!

Dad and I built it last summer. Dad sawed and hammered, and I got to hand him nails. Also, I got to pick the paint, but too bad I picked the brightest orange in the whole world! I liked the color on the can; but when it got all over the clubhouse, it was extra-bright orangey-orange.

Howie and Zack said it should be blue. I said, I know, but I didn't get to pick any more colors. I had to stay with the orange. They said too bad, but it was all right inside, because it wasn't painted in there.

The outside looked better when we painted our motto on the front with black paint like this:

Boys Are Great, and Girls Are Not Great.

Howie and Zack are the only other members of Boys Are Great. They said maybe if we tell more people about our club, we will get more members.

Howie said, "What about passing out flyers for the club?"

I told Howie and Zack about Penny's girl club flyers and how it got wrecked because of bad initials. Howie wanted to know if people would think our initials were no good too: BAG.

I said, "No, a bag is a good thing. You can carry things in it. Or you can cut holes for your head and your arms if it's a brown grocery store bag and make an Indian costume."

Howie and Zack agreed that BAG was okay. We decided instead of flyers we would decorate our notebooks with our initials, BAG. We would take them to school and put them on top of our desks. Then, when people asked why does your notebook say BAG on it, we would tell them that boys are great! Then boys would want to join, even if the clubhouse was bright orange.

Howie got some blue cloth from his mother's scrap bag for us to use. I got glue and glitter from Mom. We cut big squares of the cloth and glued them onto the front of our notebooks.

Then we wrote B and A and G with glue. We poured the glitter over the glue-letters while the glue was still wet, so the glitter would stick. After a while, we turned the notebooks over.

The extra glitter fell onto the floor, and we had supergreat notebooks that said BAG. Also, the floor looked neat with the shiny glitter sprinkled all over it.

Howie, Zack, and I were so excited about taking our notebooks to school on Monday, we could hardly stand it. We were sure our teacher, Mr. Ramirez, would like them a lot and maybe even ask if we would make him a special cover for his notebook too.

Mr. Ramirez is a man, which is the same as a boy, just older—old enough to teach second grade, which is what we're in.

On Monday, I ran to school; but when I got close, I walked slow like a snail so I could show my notebook around and people could see it. If you run, it goes by too fast and no one can see your fancy notebook cover.

I walked extra-slow into our room, which is Room 2A. My seat is in the front row, close to the chalkboard so I will pay attention better to the math problems and spelling words. I put my notebook on top of my desk, and when Mr. Ramirez came by, I said, "Look at my notebook!"

Mr. Ramirez said it looked shiny and nice.

I said, "The initials are for Boys Are Great. I have a club. Howie and Zack are in the club. Do you want a notebook cover too?"

Mr. Ramirez said that was nice of me to ask, but he thought boys and girls are both great, so his cover would have to have too many initials to fit— BAGABG—and you couldn't even pronounce it.

Howie came over with Zack. They showed their notebook covers too. Howie said, "Don't you think boys are greater than girls, Mr. Ramirez?"

Mr. Ramirez didn't think so. He said his wife was a grown-up girl, and he thought she was super-great.

Howie said it was different for grown-up ladies, but then Mr. Ramirez had to go and say that he had a little girl only four, and he thought she was great too. He said she was smart and kind and knew all her letters and could count to twenty-four.

I said, "Oh." But I think if Mr. Ramirez wasn't her very own father, he would see she wasn't all that great. I mean, she can't even get to twenty-five.

After the first day Zack and I were the only two who had the BAG notebooks. Howie said his dog tore the cover off his, but I didn't think so because it didn't have any teeth marks or dog slobber on it.

On the third day, Zack got surrounded at recess by a group of girls who started asking him math questions real real fast. He couldn't keep up! He got confused and said four plus three is two. All the girls laughed at him and walked off shouting, "Girls are greater than boys!"

On Friday, I lost the spelling bee to Melodie. I missed *decide* and she spelled that right and also one more word, *reluctant,* which is too hard a word for second grade, Mr. Ramirez said. But she got it right anyway.

On the way home, Howie, Zack, and I decided to change our club to a detective club called the Spy Guys. We would solve mysteries and find buried treasure chests.

When I got home, Penny and some other girls were in our kitchen. It smelled really good in there!

I said, "What's going on?"

Mom said it was the newly formed Fig Street Cooking Club For Young Ladies.

FSCCFYL is funny initials for a club, but I didn't say anything because it smelled good in the kitchen and I wanted some.

They were making chocolate chip cookies, but they didn't let us Spy Guys have any. Penny said it was because of my club. I told her we gave up that club and started a new one, but she still didn't let me have any of the cookies.

3
Spy Guys

For two weeks we didn't get any cases to be detectives for, so we sat around in our orange clubhouse. We yelled and pretended to have sleeping sickness. We drank Kool-Aid and ate pretzels. We thought of secret agent names we could call ourselves when we got a mystery to solve. I decided to be Super Tommy-Man.

Howie said he was going to be Howie Treasure Trapper, so we started digging a few holes in the backyard in case there was treasure buried there.

Mom said it was okay to dig, if we only dug in places where there was no grass or flowers.

She made one more rule after Dad fell into one of our holes and sprained his ankle. The new rule was we have to fill our holes up when we're finished digging them. Also we had to tell Dad sorry and make him a get-well card. We signed the card Super Tommy-Man, Howie Treasure Trapper, and Zack Mystery Master.

Penny came out while we were digging. She popped a loud snap with her pink bubble gum and said, "What are you digging for?"

And I said, "To get big arm muscles so I can beat you up." I knew she would tell Mom and I would probably have to eat extra peas, but I didn't want Penny to know there might be buried treasure out there. I wanted only us Spy Guys to find it.

Mom came out and said I shouldn't talk about beating people up even if I really did want to. I had to say sorry to Penny, but I didn't have to make a card.

Penny's cooking club kept meeting every few days and going out of the house with plates of stuff. No one brought us any. Howie thought maybe we should paint over our old slogan on the outside of the clubhouse. I said no, but he and Zack got some of the leftover orange paint from my dad and they painted out Girls Are Not Great.

I said to stop it right now, so they left the Boys Are Great part. If they had painted that out, I would have quit the club even though it's in my own backyard.

After not getting any mysteries to solve, we finally made

some flyers on the computer. We didn't use any colored words, so we would only use the black ink.

We handed Spy Guy flyers all up and down Fig Street. We made sure to tuck our shirts in and say *ma'am* and *sir* and please and *thank-you* when we passed them out. Dad says if you want to sell a product or a service you have to look nice and be pleasant; that's why.

Here's one of the flyers so you can see it:

Spy Guys

Tommy, Howie, Zack

If you have a mystery, come to the orange clubhouse in the Jackson's backyard on Fig Street.

After two weeks, like I said, we got a case. Here's what happened.

We were eating pretzels, just like every other day, and there was a knock on the clubhouse door. I opened it. It was old Mrs. Peeples! Can you

believe it? I thought our first customer would be a
kid, but Mrs. Peeples is the oldest person on our
whole street!

We were so surprised, we forgot to ask her to
come in. Instead, we jumped up, tucked in our
shirts, got real scared, and went out.

When I saw Mrs. Peeples looking at our clubhouse, I got embarrassed! It is so orange. I wished
it was blue. A really pretty blue like the sky.

"Yes, ma'am?" I said. "Can we solve a mystery for you?"

"Yes, you can, boys," old Mrs. Peeples said.

I was shaky! Maybe she heard funny noises at night and wanted us to find out what it was. Maybe we would have to stay over for a whole night being more and more scared! But it wasn't that.

"I can't find my glasses," she said. "I don't need them much, but I do need them to read the paper, and I sure want to read my paper!"

We said, "Yes, ma'am." And we followed her home.

It was okay to go into her house because Mrs. Peeples knew everyone on Fig Street. She knew me when I was born! Every year she made jars of jelly for everyone on the whole street, and she came to everyone's birthday parties even if they were only one or two years old.

When we got to her house, she sat down in her big pink chair and took some green yarn out of a basket.

"I'll just knit this shawl," she said. "I don't need glasses for knitting. No, sirree. I can knit with my eyes shut. You boys bring me those glasses when you find them."

We looked at each other like we didn't know what to do; then we started looking—very carefully, because you can't rummage through a lady's things who is almost one hundred years old. You have to be proper and neat. You don't touch anything, especially if it looks like gold or diamonds.

Zack found the glasses. They were on a shelf in Mrs. Peeples's library room.

"I could hardly see them myself," he told her.

She gave us each a dollar, and we said, "Thank you, Mrs. Peeples," and went back to the clubhouse.

"That was pretty good for the first case," Zack said.

Howie said we should put "successful" on our next set of flyers, now that we had solved a mystery. He also said we should stop yelling and having sleeping sickness, because if someone told our customers, maybe we wouldn't get any more cases.

I looked at my dollar and said, "How much does it cost to buy blue paint?"

Howie and Zack said they didn't know, maybe five dollars.

I said, "I will solve four more mysteries and then buy the paint."

I asked Dad about the paint at dinner. Dad said it would cost about fifteen dollars. I picked my broccoli to little tiny pieces until Mom said I needed to be a good boy and eat it all up.

Fourteen more mysteries were a lot. It would take years!

4
A Harder Case

It took a few weeks to get our spy business up and going, but pretty soon we had found a lost puppy, Mrs. Peeples's glasses again, and one Saturday morning we sat out by Mr. Klopper's berry bushes to see what was eating the berries off them. It was a flock of white birds—I don't know what kind—so we helped Mr. Klopper put some nets over the bushes, and he paid us two dollars each instead of our usual one dollar fee.

I was getting closer to the fifteen dollars, but then the cooking girls started selling us some treats, so I got poorer.

One day one of the girls came to our clubhouse to deliver some cookies.

It was Melodie, the spelling champion of the second grade. I wanted to be spelling champion, but Melodie was nice and she brought cookies, so we let her come in.

"Here's your cookies," she said. "Where's my money?"

"Here," I said, giving her two quarters.

"Fifty cents! Is that all?" she said.

I told her that was half of a whole fee for solving a mystery, and that made her feel better. She sat there for a while, then said, "This is a nice clubhouse," and she left.

The next day she came again with more cookies and a plant. "This place needs a woman's touch."

I told her to take the plant home, because it was a boys' clubhouse, not a flower bed, and if we wanted any plants we would go down to Pat's Hardware Store around the corner and buy them ourselves.

She said sorry in a way that didn't sound like she was, and she put the plant outside. Then she came back in and sat right down on the floor!

We didn't know what to do because girls didn't come to our clubhouse, except for Mrs. Peeples, and for her we go outside.

We looked at Melodie and then at each other, and we ate our cookies and no one said anything.

"I have a mystery for you to solve," she said finally. "But I don't have any dollars for your fee. I use my allowance for the cooking class because I want to be able to cook when I grow up and get married and have children."

That made sense to me, so I kept looking at her, but Howie butted in.

"What's your mystery?" he said. "If it's good, maybe you can pay us in cookies and pies."

"I'll give you a whole pie if you can solve it," she said. Then she started to cry, which all of us didn't like one teeny little bit. "Nobody can find my grandpa!" she said.

It was true. Melodie's grandpa was missing. It was in the newspaper the very next morning, with his picture on the front page and everything. The paper said his name was Mr. Olin Bounty, he was seventy-nine years old, and he had a sickness called Old Timers which made him forget things like where he was or if you were his friend.

Melodie wasn't at school that day, so I won the spelling bee with *dinosaur,* because I remembered the *aur* part at the end.

Even though I won, I was sad the whole day and kept wondering if the Spy Guys could find someone the police and firemen couldn't even find.

We all hurried to the clubhouse after school. Melodie was there waiting for us, and she was still crying!

"Tell us about your grandpa," I said. "That'll help us look for him."

"He likes to take long walks," she said, sniffling. "He likes pizza. He likes to take me to the park after school and watch me ride my bike."

"Let's go to the park right now," Zack said. "Maybe he forgot he was lost and is meeting you there like always."

So we went, but he wasn't there. Melodie cried more, but I told her to stop. "If you stop crying, you don't have to give me a pie."

That didn't help, so I told her if she didn't stop crying, we would quit working on the case. So she stopped. Then she looked and she screamed, "Grandpa! Grandpa!!!" and ran as fast as she could toward him.

There he was with her grandma. She had found him up in the attic sleeping on his old army cot.

Melodie threw herself at old Mr. Olin Bounty like
a dog throws himself on his master. It was nice.

We guys turned around and went home, because
the case was over.

"I'm glad that one's over," Zack said. "It was
too serious for us. We need to stick to finding
thieves and digging up lost treasure chests full of
gold."

"That's for sure," I said. "No more lost people.
Too scary."

"Too much crying," said Howie.

Melodie came by the next day with a chocolate pie, which we tried to pay her for since we didn't solve the case, but she said, no way, it was free because we tried so hard and because her grandpa was safe and she didn't want us to tell people she cried so much.

I told her I would cry if my grandpa was lost. She asked if he had Old Timers and I said no, but he has allergies.

5
A Girl in the Club

After that Melodie wanted to join the club. Howie and Zack said okay, but I said no, she couldn't join, not in a bajillion years! I said the club was for boys only, no girls allowed.

Zack said Melodie made the best cookies in the world and if she was a Spy Guy, maybe we wouldn't have to pay. Howie said if I didn't have to pay for treats, maybe I could save enough money to buy paint to cover up the orange.

Finally I agreed she could join, but only if she would say the motto.

We told her to come on Wednesday to the meeting, and we would let her in. But on Wednesday when she came, I said, "You can't be a Spy Guy, because you're not a guy. You're a girl."

She said a girl could too be a spy or even president of the United States of America.

I said I didn't think that was going to happen because girls cry too much. She got mad at me and said I was making fun of her because she cried when her grandpa was lost.

I said, "Sorry, that's not what I meant, but I still don't think a lady can be the president, because I just don't think so."

Zack said, "Melodie can be a Spy Guy. Everybody stand up." So we all stood up. Zack said, "Put your hand over your heart." We all did that, like we were going to say the Pledge. Then he said, "Okay, Melodie, say the motto."

And Melodie said, "Boys are great, and girls are great too."

That's how we got a girl in our club and also how we got our motto changed. Dad helped me paint the new motto on the clubhouse on Saturday.

I asked Dad about the president thing and he said, "Yes, son, a woman could become president," so the next time Melodie came to our meeting, I let her have my seat because it's the best one. That way, if she is president someday, she'll remember I was nice to her and let me visit her in the White House.

6
Girls Everywhere

After a few days we had to split up into two clubs. A lot of girls came to join now that we had a new motto, but they wanted to be detectives about different things than we boys did.

We wanted to dig up treasure chests that had been left by one-legged pirates, but Melodie said pirates didn't leave anything in our state because there wasn't any ocean close by and it was too heavy to carry boatloads of gold very far even if you had two legs.

The girls wanted to do spy things like find out if Barry likes Tasha, but don't tell anyone except our club.

The boys didn't care about that at all! We decided the girls could have their club, and we could have ours. Melodie said they still got to use the clubhouse, and my mom said that was okay, so what happened was the boys got kicked out of our very own clubhouse every Thursday.

I said it wasn't fair for the girls to kick me out of my own clubhouse even for one day of the week, but Dad said I had to share things even if I really really loved them, like I loved my clubhouse. Besides, Penny had joined the girls' half of Spy Guys, and it wouldn't be nice to cut my own sister out of the club.

That sounded right, so I stopped complaining. Plus on the days the girls had club, I got my homework done faster.

Mr. Ramirez said for homework we have to do a report about our favorite president, plus draw a picture of him. I drew Abraham Lincoln because I liked his tall hat and beard. Also because he was tall and skinny and you could make him out of a

stick man, which is what I can draw.

7
Loud and Lazy
Uncle Mick

The scariest thing that happened all through second grade was when Melodie's grandpa was missing. But another scary thing happened that was superscary too!

A whole bunch of us Spy Guys and Spy Girls were sitting in the orange clubhouse. I was trying to convince everyone to chip in some quarters for new paint, but the girls said no; they liked it, and they wanted to paint big yellow flowers all over it.

Some girls said, "Flowers, flowers, flowers!"

And I said, "No flowers! No flowers!" I said it so loud I was yelling!

It was like a fight starting, but suddenly there was a loud knock on the door, and we all got totally quiet. What if a customer with a mystery heard us shouting at each other?

I tucked in my shirt and went to open the door, because if it's Mrs. Peeples, I don't want to look sloppy.

It wasn't Mrs. Peeples. Instead there was a big man standing there. I didn't know him. He was a stranger. I am not supposed to talk to strangers.

He said, "Is this the clubhouse of Thomas Arthur Jackson?"

I said, "Yes. Who are you?"

All the kids were saying, "Who is it?"

I turned around to them and said, "I don't know. It's a great big man."

Penny came up to the door and stood beside me. She said, "Who are you and what do you want?"

He said, "You must be Penelope Amanda Jackson."

She said, "That does it, Mister. Tell us who you are or we're going to call the police!"

The big man started to laugh. He laughed and laughed and laughed. He got louder and louder, and that's when I realized who it was!

"You're Uncle Mick," I said. "You're loud and lazy!"

"Loud and lazy?" he shouted. "Who told you that?"

"Our mother," said Penny.

By this time all the other kids had crowded behind us at the door. They said things like, "Who is he?" and "Why does he laugh so much?"

"Now that's a woman I want to see!" he said. "Where is my beautiful sister, Melinda Suzanne Plummer Jackson?"

Penny said she'd go and get Mom. I think she was afraid of Uncle Mick and wanted to get away from him. I wasn't afraid of him after he started laughing, but I still wouldn't let him in the clubhouse.

I said, "Why didn't you go to the house first?"

And he said the orange of the clubhouse was so brilliant he was drawn to it. "It was like a magnet pulling me in," he said. "I'm sorry if I scared you."

I said it was okay, no problem. But I didn't invite him in. I said we could sit outside until Mom came. The other kids sat outside with us.

Uncle Mick told jokes about penguins and alligators. Then he told a joke about a clubhouse that was so orange it turned into a pumpkin and got made into a pie. I said, "Hey, that's my clubhouse you're talking about!"

He told jokes that were so funny, Elizabeth, one of the Spy Girls, laughed so hard she got hiccups and couldn't stop no matter if we scared her or surprised her or made her hold her breath.

Just then Mom came running out of the house.

"Mick!" she said.

He said, "Melinda!"

They threw themselves into a big hug. They hugged and hugged and hugged!

"The kids tell me I'm loud and lazy," he said. "I wonder where they got that idea."

"I wonder if you got a job yet," Mom said. "If you did, maybe I won't call you lazy anymore, little brother!"

"Yep," he said. "I got myself a great job. I'll tell you all about it over dinner. I'm staying for dinner. Is that okay?"

"That's great," I said. "Stay all week! Stay forever!"

8
Uncle Mick

For dinner that night we had a celebration. Mom said she couldn't believe that Uncle Mick was here. She hadn't seen him in two years, and he hadn't even called up to say he was coming.

"I wanted to surprise you," he said.

"You certainly did that," Mom said.

I said, "How loud are you? Are you really lazy? Do you have sleeping sickness? Does sleeping sickness hurt?"

Uncle Mick said, "Look at this, Tommy," so I looked. He took a spoonful of mashed potatoes and made a mustache on his lip.

I laughed and tried to make one for me, but Mom said, "Thomas Arthur," so I licked it off. But I smiled at Uncle Mick, and he winked at me.

Dad and Mom and Uncle Mick stayed up late. They made a pot of coffee, and I heard Dad say, "Tell us about your new job, Mick," as I was going upstairs to do my homework. Subtracting was for tonight. Ten minus one. Ten minus two. Ten minus three. I can do all the ten minuses. Then I did the nines up to nine minus nine.

I wanted to know all about Uncle Mick, but instead I went to bed. I had to wait all the way until the next afternoon. Uncle Mick met me at school and said we could walk to the ice-cream shop if I didn't mind. I said, "Yes!"

When we sat down to eat our double-scoops, I said, "Are you going to live on Fig Street now?"

He said just for a while because he was going to Africa to build houses for poor people. He was also

going to teach people to read if they didn't know
how already.

I said that sounded like fun and I wanted to go
to Africa too. He said first I have to finish second
grade and third grade and all the way up to twelfth
grade!

"I wish you were staying," I said. "You're
funny. But so far you aren't very loud."

"I'm not loud anymore," he said. "I grew up."

"What about the lazy part?" I asked. I took a bite out of the ice cream—a great big bite instead of licking—and it made my teeth hurt!

"I used to be lazy," he said, "really horribly lazy." He took a few licks of his ice-cream cone because it was melting down the sides.

"When I was in school, I was so lazy I never did my homework. After a while, I never did my work in class either. I just stared at the clock on the wall."

I said, "Mr. Ramirez would send me to the office if I did that."

Uncle Mick said, "I know. I used to get sent to Mr. B.'s office all the time!"

I said, "Who is Mr. B.?"

Uncle Mick said, "He was the principal."

And I said, "Oh."

On the way home, we stopped by Mrs. Peeples's house. Uncle Mick wanted to give her a pint of ice cream. "Vanilla is her favorite," he said.

"How do you know that?" My mouth was hanging wide open. Did he know Mrs. Peeples?

"She was my fifth grade teacher," he said, "right here at Fig Street Elementary."

"You grew up here?" I said.

He said, "Yep, right in the very house you live in. Your mom never told you?"

I said, "No, she didn't!"

When Mrs. Peeples saw Uncle Mick, she smiled and her face was crinkly and happy. "Michael Plummer!" she said. "I just knew you would turn out well!"

"I have turned out well, Mrs. Peeples," he said, "and I have brought you some ice cream because you are so sweet."

Mrs. Peeples laughed and said thank you. She invited us in, but Uncle Mick said we needed to get home. I asked her if she needed any help finding her glasses; but then I saw they were right on her face, and I felt extra-silly!

9
A Big Mistake

I had saved up to eight dollars, which was half
way to my gallon of paint, but Melodie had an idea
that ended up costing me all my money. Here's
what happened.

Melodie said it was our duty as young citizens
to do good things for our community. She said
we should get together and do good deeds to help
people on our street. She said it didn't matter if the
people were nice or not.

She said if we were nice, maybe they would
be nice too. Pretty soon everyone would be nice,
even scary people like Mr. Bolt. He lives in the big

house on the corner and never sits on the porch to wave.

I said, "Not Mr. Bolt. I'm not going there."

Melodie said okay, but we would go to all the other houses for sure.

So on Saturday we all met at the clubhouse. There were five girls and three boys, which makes eight of us altogether. We decided to go all in one group because it's less scary if there's more of you, and Melodie would do all the talking. Then if the person wanted us to do a good deed for them, we would all do it.

We started at my house because that's where we were. Melodie told us to stand up straight, and she would ring the doorbell.

I said we didn't need to ring the doorbell. It was my own house!

But Melodie said no, we had to do things right or not do them at all.

My dad came to the door and looked at us funny. "Yes?" he said. "Is there something you kids need?"

"We are doing good deeds on Fig Street today, Mr. Jackson," Melodie said. "Can we do a good deed for you?"

My dad stood there for a second, scratching his nose, like he was trying to think of something for us to do. Then he said, "Yes. I want you to trot right down to the end of the street. You know lonely Mr. Bolt in the last house? Knock on his door, and ask him what you can do for him. Got it?"

Melodie said, "Yes, sir," but I looked at my dad funny. Didn't he know Mr. Bolt was a scary old man?

Dad said, "Go on, trot on down there."

Melodie made us trot. The rest of us wanted to just walk, but Melodie said part of doing the good deed is to do it just how you're asked and since my dad had said "trot" to the corner, then we had to. Trotting is running, but slower.

When we got to Mr. Bolt's house, I stood next to Penny because even though she's just a girl and sometimes she plays tricks on me, she would take care of me if Mr. Bolt liked to eat little children or wanted to kidnap us and keep us in the attic in cages.

"Whatcha want?" Mr. Bolt said. "I don't buy cookies."

"We want to do a good deed for you, sir," Melodie said.

"I don't need any," he said. He started to close the door, but Melodie stepped in closer and said, "Please, Mr. Bolt, we'd really like to help out, if there's something we can do for you. Really."

Mr. Bolt opened the door and stared at all eight of us for a long time.

He stared at us so long I wondered if we should go home and forget about doing good deeds. Then he said, "Well, truth is, I've got some weeds that need to be picked. Come on."

We walked after him to his backyard, and he showed us the place. It was covered up with lots of weeds.

"Used to be pretty back here," he said. "But I let it go, since my wife died. Most of the yard is a real mess. Maybe you can pick out these weeds."

He walked away from us and banged the back door shut.

"Come on, guys," Melodie said, so we all got down on our knees and started picking weeds and weeds and weeds.

After we finished with the part Mr. Bolt had shown us, Zack said, "Look over here at these weeds," and we looked.

It was another patch of stuff that looked pretty scruffy like it wanted to be picked.

"Should we do this section too?" we asked Melodie.

She said, "Yep, absolutely, let's make it perfect. He's sad his wife died. Maybe this will cheer him up."

We picked and picked and picked and picked, and pretty soon the whole place was picked clean.

Which is when Mr. Bolt came out of the house. We jumped up when we saw him, wiped our dirty, dirty hands on our clothes and smiled. "Well?" Melodie said. "How do you like it, Mr. Bolt?"

Mr. Bolt didn't say anything. I thought, I bet he's so happy we did this for him he's going to invite us in for hot dogs and potato chips!

"Well," he said slowly. "I'd like it a whole lot better if you hadn't picked my one little flower bed clean out." Then he shook his head three times, clucked at us sadly, turned around, and went in the house again. The door slammed loudly behind him.

Penny sat down on the grass and started to cry. It took about ten seconds before Melodie did the same thing, and then the rest of the girls did too. Elizabeth cried and hiccuped at the same time.

We boys stood there with our dirty hands in our pockets. I stood on my left foot, then on my right foot. I didn't know what we were supposed to do.

We didn't do anything for a long time. Just stood there, girls crying, boys standing. Then we left and went home. Nobody said anything. Nobody knew what to do.

I thought of the answer that night in bed. The next day, I called everyone on the phone and said, "Come to the clubhouse, and bring all your money."

Everyone came, and we put all our money on the floor in a big pile.

When we counted it up, it was thirty-seven dollars. Eight of the dollars were mine.

"Let's go," I said. We walked in a long sad line down to Pat's Hardware Store, and we asked the man where the flowers were and how many we could buy for thirty-seven dollars.

The man said we could buy some flowers, but if we wanted to buy seeds for flowers, it wouldn't be nearly as much money.

"No," Melodie said. "We need to buy flowers, so he doesn't have to wait long to see the pretty blooms. The pretty flowers will cheer him up."

The flowers were fifty-nine cents, so we bought sixty flowers. I ran home and got my old red wagon from when I was little out of the garage. We put all the flowers in there in their little plastic pots, and we wheeled them to Mr. Bolt's house.

"Should we ask him first, or just sneak back and plant them for him?" Howie asked.

"We will ask him," Melodie said, and I agreed. He didn't need any more surprises about his flower bed.

"What do you do-gooders want now?" Mr. Bolt said. "Are you going to dig up my mailbox today? Or my lawn? Maybe you can dig up the whole house!"

Melodie was the leader, so she did the talking. "We know that what we did was terrible, Mr. Bolt.

We didn't mean to hurt your feelings. We were trying to help. So we brought these for you." She mo-
tioned for the wagon, and I pulled it around where
he could see it better.

He looked at the wagon full of pretty flowers.
Then he looked at us, but he didn't say anything.
He bit his bottom lip and said, "Hmmm."

"We used our money from solving mysteries," I
said.

He still didn't say anything, so I started to think
he hated the flowers we bought and wanted something different which would be terrible because
we'd used all the money we had.

Elizabeth started to hiccup, but she kept really
quiet about it and didn't cry.

"Well, Mr. Bolt," Melodie said, "may we plant
these for you?"

"Yeah, sure," he said. "But let me show you where. And how. I don't want you kids messing anything else up back there!"

Mr. Bolt got down on his hands and knees and showed us with a little spade how to dig holes four inches deep. "And keep the plants about four inches apart too, because they'll grow, and they might get too crowded."

We took turns digging and passing the plants from the wagon to the flower plot. Mr. Bolt sat on the ground with his legs crossed and chewed on a piece of grass while he watched us. It was almost creepy, and I decided right there I wasn't going to do any more good deeds because this one had turned out so bad and so expensive.

When we finished planting sixty plants, Mr. Bolt got up and turned on the water hose. "Clean your hands up," he said. "Leave the watering to me. I don't want you to drown my new flowers."

We washed our hands and then wiped them dry on our dirty clothes. Then we turned to go out the gate. I couldn't wait to leave. I wanted my mom and dad.

"Stop," Mr. Bolt said.

We turned slowly to look at him, and I thought he was going to say, "I don't like this kind of flower. Dig them all up and take them back where they came from." But he said something different.

"This is the nicest thing anyone's done for me since Harriet died," he said. "Thank you, kids."

"You're welcome," we all said.

I breathed a big breath and even smiled a little.

Then we started to laugh, and we ran out of the gate and all the way back to the clubhouse.

10
A Picnic for Mrs. Peeples

It was Melodie's mom, Mrs. Bounty, who got the idea of having a Fig Street birthday party for Mrs. Peeples.

Mrs. Bounty said, "It's only fair that after all the jelly she's made for us over the years, and all her other simple kindnesses, we should honor her in this way. After all, she's going to be eighty-seven years old!"

I told Mrs. Bounty that I didn't think the party was a great idea, because eighty-seven is so old you might die blowing out all the candles. But Mrs. Bounty laughed and said Mrs. Peeples was at the peak of health and would probably live to be one hundred years old. I figured out that was thirteen more years. By then I would be seven plus thirteen which is twenty! I went around shouting, "Twenty! Twenty!" until Dad said it was time to be a quiet seven-year-old.

On Saturday, we drove to the park for the party. Even though the park is close, we drove because we had to bring so much stuff. We had to bring folding tables and chairs and macaroni salad and ten pounds of steaks and mustard and soda pop and lemon bars.

We crammed three in the back, which was squishy. Usually it's just me and Penny in the back seat, but this time Uncle Mick was there too.

Every person from Fig Street was at the picnic, because everyone loves Mrs. Peeples.

The park was crowded with lots of people setting up tables. There were tables where you could throw a ring over a bottle and win a yo-yo. You didn't even have to pay a quarter to try. All the games were free because Mrs. Peeples said not to bring presents, but to have games for the children.

The Spy Girls had a table for selling cookies. It was five cookies for a dollar, and all the money goes to help a little girl in Guatemala. Her name is Maria, and she is an orphan. That means she doesn't have a mom or a dad or anyone to take care of her. Guatemala is somewhere very far away, which I will learn about next year in third grade when I learn the countries.

The Spy Guys didn't have a table, but we did pass out our Spy Guys cards to all the people. We told everyone if you don't have any mysteries, we will pick your weeds instead, but please show us which plants are weeds and which are flowers, so we don't make a mistake again.

Mrs. Peeples sat in her rocking chair under a great big tree. If she sits on a blanket on the ground, she can't get up, and she'll still be there when it gets dark and the bugs come out.

Everyone took turns going over to hug her and get a kiss from her and tell her happy birthday. I asked her if she was feeling okay since she was eighty-seven now, and she said she was feeling better than ever.

"I feel so good, I might even start solving mysteries with you boys!" she said. Then she squeezed my hand and winked at me, so I don't think she really wants to join our club; but if she comes over, I won't tell her no, because she's a very old lady, and she can do whatever she wants.

Mrs. Peeples likes the Spy Guys. I know because about once a week she calls us to look for her glasses. But the glasses are not really lost. I know because every time we go, there is ice cream in bowls on the counter, and her glasses are always in the same place they were the first time.

After I got kissed by Mrs. Peeples, something happened that scared me.

The bad thing that happened was this: Uncle Mick was helping me pass out Spy Guys cards. He would walk up to anyone and say, "Do you have a minute for my nephew to give you his business card?"

He was so nice that everyone said yes, and then I would give them the card and tell them about the mysteries and the weeds.

But then, all of a sudden, one man started to shout, "You're that no-good loud and lazy Michael Pumpkin!"

At first I laughed because nobody's name is really *Michael Pumpkin*, but then I looked real close and saw that the shouting man was Mr. Olin Bounty, Melodie's grandpa.

I thought maybe he was getting sick from his disease and was talking real loud but not making any sense. I hoped Uncle Mick wouldn't laugh at him or call him a crazy old man.

But Uncle Mick didn't laugh. He got real quiet. Then he walked up to Mr. Olin Bounty and held out his hand for shaking hands.

"Hello, Mr. Bounty," he said. "It's nice to see you again. My name's Michael Plummer. Everyone calls me Mick."

"I'm not going to shake your hand. No, sir," said Mr. Bounty. "You sat in my office too many times!"

That's when I realized that Mr. Bounty was Mr. B., the principal Uncle Mick used to get sent to all the time!

"Please, Mr. B.," Uncle Mick said, "I'm so sorry for being such a bad student. I really am sorry. I hope you'll forgive me."

Melodie ran over and stood by her grandpa. "It's okay, Grandpa," she said. "Come over here."

"You are a disgrace to this community," Mr. Bounty said to Uncle Mick.

Lots of people were gathered around us now. Uncle Mick was real red in the face. Any redder and maybe he would have caught on fire!

"In my younger days, I was very foolish," Uncle Mick said.

"Foolish, hah!" Mr. Bounty said. "You skipped school. You yelled in class. You flunked out! You ruined our perfect record of having all our students graduate."

I pulled on Uncle Mick's sleeve. "You dropped out of high school?"

Mr. Bounty started to walk away with Melodie.

"Wait, Mr. B.," said Uncle Mick. "I want to tell you that I did finish high school."

"You did?" Mr. Bounty turned around. He walked back to Uncle Mick. "Are you telling me the truth, Mr. Pumpkin?"

"Yes, sir." Uncle Mick smiled. "I had to take night classes for two years, but I finished and I have a diploma."

Mr. Bounty smiled; then he shouted real loud, "He finished high school. Michael Pumpkin finished high school!"

Uncle Mick looked embarrassed, but I could tell that he was happy that Mr. Bounty was so happy. They shook hands. Then they hugged.

"Every student finishes at Fig Street High!" Mr. Bounty said.

Then Mr. Olin Bounty turned to me and said, "Young man, your uncle is an inspiration to us all.

He finished the job even though it was hard for him. Remember that."

I said I would remember it. Then Mr. Bounty and Melodie held hands and walked back to their picnic table.

Uncle Mick said, "I need a walk. Come on." He and I walked around the whole park. He told me how he was bad in school and how he didn't listen to his teachers. He told me how hard it was to get a job when he hadn't finished high school. He said I should try my best to finish high school well. I said I would try as hard as I could!

After our walk, we stopped at Mr. Klopper's table. He was giving away slices of berry pies. "Berries right from my bushes," he said.

Even Mr. Bolt had a table. He was giving away hot dogs to everyone. They were free even if you wanted ketchup or mustard or both. I was still a little bit afraid of Mr. Bolt, but the hot dogs were free, so I made myself get brave enough to go over there.

"Both," I said when he asked about the ketchup and mustard. Uncle Mick got a plain one, and then he started talking to Mr. Bolt about foot-long hot dogs and which is better—all beef or all meat—and why are they called "dogs" anyway, because they don't have teeth or tails or fur.

They were talking so much about hot dogs that I finally walked away. I found Melodie and her grandpa and sat down with them.

I played a game of checkers with Mr. Bounty. Sometimes he made a wrong move, but I didn't say anything about it because he's very old, and he needs all us kids to be extra-nice to him.

Also, if I said, "Mr. Bounty, that's cheating," then Melodie would cry and say he wasn't cheating, but that he sometimes forgets what the moves are.

Melodie leaned over to tell me something quietly in my ear.

"I learned it's called Alzheimer's disease."

"What is?" I said.

"Old Timers is really called Alzheimer's disease."

I said I would try to remember to say it right, but to not get mad at me if I forgot because it was a hard word. I also made her promise not to ask Mr. Ramirez to put it on our spelling bee list, and she said okay.

Then Melodie's mom called to everyone to gather around Mrs. Peeples. A great big birthday cake came out. It was all covered up in pink frosting and eighty-seven candles! Some men put it on a table. Everyone stood around in a great big circle with only Mrs. Peeples at the table by the cake.

Someone started to sing and in about one second everyone was singing, "Happy Birthday to you!" to Mrs. Peeples. She cried and laughed at the same time, and then she took many tries before she blew out all the candles. Everyone clapped for her while she huffed and puffed and blew them all out!

We all got cake and ice cream, and we all kissed Mrs. Peeples again and said, "Many more happy years to you," and then we went home.

11
Proud of Me

That night my whole family sat in the living room. We ate popcorn and talked about the day. I said I was glad Mrs. Peeples had enough breath to blow out all her candles. Uncle Mick said he was leaving in two weeks for Africa.

"Are you ever coming back?" I said. I didn't look at him, because I was sad he was leaving. I wanted him to stay forever.

"I'll be back in two years. You'll be nine. We'll have ice cream, and we'll ride bikes all over this town. Maybe I'll run for mayor!"

Dad said we should all clap and cheer for Mick, because he was doing something so decent and so good. We all stood up and clapped and cheered. I ran over and gave Uncle Mick a hug.

I said, "I can't wait to be nine."

Mom said she'd been thinking about how Uncle Mick was going to go to Africa to help people. Mom said that she wanted to do something to help people too.

"So I'm going to be doing Mr. Bolt's shopping and housecleaning. And Dad's going to help him fix up his place."

Penny said we should clap and cheer for Mom and Dad, so we did that too. Then I said we should clap and cheer for Penny for sending money to Maria in Guatemala, so we did.

Then it got quiet. I felt silly. Everyone else had done something good that could be clapped for, but I hadn't done anything good.

Then Dad said, "Let's all cheer and clap for Tommy, because he took his little club of three boys and turned it into a wonderful club that helps people all over Fig Street. You did a good job."

Everyone cheered and clapped. I was really happy.

Then Uncle Mick said, "I want to do something for the club, something extra-special, because I've had such a wonderful time while I was here."

He looked at me and Penny. He thought and thought. Then he smacked his head with his hand and said, "I know what I'll do! I'll buy some paint, and we'll paint that clubhouse any color you want."

Dad and Mom said that was the best idea they'd ever heard. Penny asked if all the kids could help with the painting part. I was so excited I couldn't say anything. I just jumped up and down and opened my eyes so wide they hurt! No more orange!

I shouted, "Blue, blue, blue, blue, blue," until Mom said, "Okay, how about blue?" and everyone laughed.

Then I ran around the whole room and said good night to everyone. I said, "I have sleeping sickness! I'm going to bed right now."

Mom said I could stay up if I wanted, but I said I was going right to sleep, because then tomorrow would come superfast and we could start painting the clubhouse!

When I got under my covers, I was so excited I couldn't sleep at all. All I could think of was my clubhouse, and how tomorrow it was going to be better than ever.

About the Author

Sharon Hambrick has had a lifelong interest in writing, and she often has three or four stories in the works. Her books introduce readers to a wide variety of characters from the veteran missionary Adoniram Judson to the children who live on Fig Street.

She and her husband have four children, a never-ending supply of story ideas. Mrs. Hambrick enjoys reading and snorkeling—just not at the same time.